TURTLE DREAM

Collected Stories from the
Hopi, Navajo, Pueblo, and
Havasupai People

Written by Gerald Hausman
Illustrated by Sid Hausman

A Mariposa Book

Published by
Mariposa Publishing
922 Baca Street
Santa Fe, New Mexico 87501
(505) 988-5582

FIRST EDITION 1989

ISBN 0-933553-06-4

for Mimi and Sid

Also from Mariposa Publishing

Children's Literature
By Joe Hayes:

The Day It Snowed Tortillas
Tales from Spanish New Mexico

Coyote &
Native American Folk Tales

The Checker Playing Hound Dog
Tall Tales from
A Southwestern Storyteller

A Heart Full of Turquoise
Pueblo Indian Tales

Adult Literature

Sweet Salt, A Novel
By Robert Mayer

TABLE OF CONTENTS

Turquoise Horse

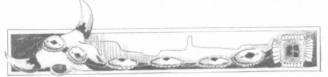

S ome years ago, in Navajo country, there was a girl
named Lisa Todachine whose father was a silversmith.

When Lisa was twelve years old, she had a dream
in which she chased a horse. She was on foot in the
dream, and the horse raced ahead of her, dancing on
small delicate hooves.

The dream came again and again. During the day
Lisa did not think about the dream, nor did she mention
it to anyone. But at night, before she went to sleep, she
remembered the horse, and it made her sad to think
that though she saw the horse every night, her dream
was always in black and white.

There came a night when the dream changed into
color. Lisa was running along a narrow trail upon a vast
mesa and the horse was ahead of her, its mane flashing

in the wind, its fore-hooves striking sparks on the hard-packed earth.

When it happened she was not surprised but pleased. The horse reared magnificently on a rock outcropping, and then, in a blaze of blue it transformed into a turquoise horse. The moment this happened Lisa knew she was in a dream, because in real life there is no such thing as blue horses. And then the horse did a wonderful thing. Rearing over the verge, it suddenly leaped into the open, empty air and, pawing miraculously, found its footing in the sky. Then it whinnied triumphantly and galloped off across the clouds.

The next morning Lisa went to where her father worked on his jewelry behind their hogan. In the warm seasons, summer and fall, he usually did his work under a four-post juniper shelter, the upper latias of which were spindly bark-peeled branches. Shadows fell in clean lines at his feet. He worked in the cool of this outdoor workshop until, little by little, the sun grew bolder, and bolder and stole all the way into the shadow of the shelter.

Lisa liked to watch her father work. His composure seemed cast of the same fire-blackened silver as his bracelets, rings and pins. He was a man of mud and fire, blood and bone whose surface was etched and hammered by years of sun and rain. He knew what it meant to make a mould and what it meant, as a grown man, to have been moulded by nature.

Lisa knew that her father was wise. She also knew that he was certain of the old ways that had been taught to him by his own father. From father to son, mother to daughter the teachings came down, year after year, sun after moon.

"Father," Lisa said, "I have a dream to tell you."

She waited while he removed a casting from the hot coals before which, holding iron tongs in a pair of heavy cowhide gloves, he sat back on the heels of his elk moccasins.

"Yes," he said, finally. "Tell me your dream."

"There is a horse. I run after it but I can never catch it. Mostly the horse is dark because I dream this dream in black and white. But last night, for the first time, the horse looked me in the eyes. I heard it snort loudly before it turned turquoise and galloped away into the clouds. Father, I need to know what this dream means, for I have it every night."

Lisa's father said nothing, nor did he look into his

daughter's worried face. He bent over his tufa-casting and tapped it with a little hammer.

Lisa knew that her father was not ignoring her. He was not, as it appeared, concentrating only on his work. He was, she knew, thinking deeply about what she had told him.

Then he got slowly to his feet and stretched his arms.

"You get stiff in that position," he said, then, "Come with me for a moment, Lisa."

Together, they walked on the dry wash just below where her father worked. A little ribbon of water, sky-colored, shivered between the clay banks that rose above their shoulders.

After walking for a few minutes, her father stopped.

"I think it was here," he said. "Yes, I am certain of it, here."

"What?" Lisa asked.

"I was your age, maybe a little younger when I made the discovery. Do you see where the water runs down from high up on the hill? Where there is now a dry scar on that cliff?"

Lisa nodded. In rainy times, such soft eroded places sang full-throated with tumbling water. If you were not careful, when the water ran at its fullest, you could be swept to your death.

"When I was your age," Lisa's father began, "I was caught in one of those sudden storms. The whole hillside seemed to come down on my head. I got swept away. A big juniper branch saved my life. I held onto it for all I was worth. When my grandfather pulled me to safety, we both stopped in our tracks. For directly in front of us was a ruined grave, one that the wild waters had ripped apart. There was silver everywhere, for as you know, the dear possessions of the dead are buried with the body."

Lisa's father turned on his moccasined heel and began to walk back to his workshop on the hill above the arroyo.

"What does this mean, Father?" she asked.

"In all that silver, there was a bracelet, that even now after all the years, I remember as if it were yesterday. The silversmith had made that bracelet a hundred years ago, and yet it was as new as the day he measured the wrist that wore it . . . a wrist that was once flesh and bone, a wrist that is now dust."

"What did you do with the bracelet?"

Looking at his daughter for the first time, Lisa's father smiled a little crookedly. She knew what that meant. Trouble. A lesson. She had said something wrong.

"You know it is a bad thing to disturb the sacred places of burial. I did nothing with the bracelet. I merely looked at it. I took it with my eyes, for a moment, and held it there. Then my grandfather and I walked on and we erased that place from our memory. It is only now, as you told me of your dream, that I remembered."

"That gravesite," Lisa said, "was ruined in the rain. You didn't know where the real location of the grave was, only where the jewelry turned up at your feet."

"That is right."

"Then why couldn't you take it and give it a proper home? Otherwise it could've been taken by someone less than yourself, a thief perhaps."

"To take that which does not belong to you, no matter the circumstance, is a bad thing. Let the runner run, the walker walk, and the thief thieve. You can't change that which is—the rain, the run-off, the broken grave. We didn't touch that silverwork. Perhaps it's still there, perhaps not. It doesn't matter. What is important is that we saw the bracelet with our eyes. . .we embraced it. From that moment on, I knew I would be a silversmith."

"But how did you know?"

"I knew because I understood—having almost drowned—that only those things which live are worth living for."

Lisa said, "I understand now."

"There is something else," her father said kneeling before his dwindling fire. "The thing that made the bracelet so beautiful was the turquoise horse that decorated it. I've never forgotten that horse that seemed to be dancing on a cloud."

Lisa waited for him to say something more, but he busied himself with his casting.

That night Lisa dreamed the dream of the turquoise horse, and again, she saw it in color. This time the horse danced upon a cloud, just as her father had said, and it beckoned her to follow. She was afraid. Backing away from the edge of the great cliff where the horse had taken its swift leap into the air, she felt fear in her throat.

"I can't come with you," she said to the horse, "I

can't walk on air."

Then the horse galloped to the mesa, and kneeling as her father had knelt before the fire, it bowed its head. Lisa had only to take one step and she would be on its back. She hesitated, and then heard the voice that came from the clouds.

The voice said, "The turquoise horse is yours now."

It was a command and Lisa obeyed.

The horse got to its feet and in one graceful bound, tossing its neck to the east, it dropped off the cliff like falling water. Then it flailed its hooves on the air, parted the clouds, swam up into the sky.

Lisa clung to the horse's mane, but she did not feel fearful. Easily, dreamily, like flowing silk, she let the horse have its head. And the horse plunged higher into the cliffs of cloud and was swallowed up.

Then she felt her body melt as the vapors wrapped her round, and the voice of the cloud-person spoke again.

Lisa could see nothing, for the mist was everywhere. She felt the gleaming flank muscle of the turquoise horse. This was real, she told herself, the voice of the cloud-person was real.

Then the world, the universe stood still, the clouds froze and everything turned into still-life.

"Hear me," the cloud-person said, "I am of the family of the Sun. The horse you ride on belongs to us. But we do not own him. No one can own the Turquoise Horse."

Lisa woke with a start. It was morning, the weekend was over and it was time to get dressed for school. The dream she'd been having dissolved in her waking mind. She got dressed, put her books in her bookbag, and had breakfast with her mother and father. They ate in silence. Morning was quiet time. It was not necessary to speak. Instead they listened.

At school Lisa remained quiet. In little bits throughout the morning her dream returned, giving her no peace. It was only after lunch, after she had gone running several miles with her friends, that she realized how tired she was, how her dream had physically drained her.

Back in the classroom, her teacher introduced a folksinger, a man with a handlebar mustache who had been assigned to their school district by the Arizona Commission on the Arts. He walked about the room, plunking a banjo and urging the children to write verses of a song that all of them would compose together.

She liked the tune and the verses rolled out, tinkly and funny, and they made her forget her dream. All the students in the room were laughing and the mustached man made his banjo ring: "Put your head on the floor, pick it up, pick it up; put your head on the floor, pick it up, pick it up."

Lisa could not help smiling at this man who was all smiles himself. Although he was not Navajo, there was something Indian about him. He didn't act like a white person. Like her father, he was sure of something. That something was inside the tight white drum head of his banjo.

If only she were sure. . . if only she had something she were certain of. . . the banjo rang for the last time. Then it was time for the students to write their own composition, something of their own, which the mustache-man would put to music for the following day.

Lisa wasn't going to write anything. She doodled on the creamy sheet of paper that covered her desktop. But her doodling, mindless and abstract, changed into something else. She began to draw the turquoise horse.

The moment she saw its image drawn by her own hand
on paper, she heard the words of the cloud-person.

> I am the Sun's son.
> I sit upon a turquoise horse
>   at the opening
>   of the sky.

> My horse walks
>   on the upper circle
>   of the rainbow.

> My horse has a sunbeam
> for a bridle.

> My horse circles
>   all the people
>   of the earth.

> Today, I, Lisa Todachine, ride
> upon his broad back
> and he is mine.

> Tomorrow
> he will belong to another.

The drawing and the words came out of her so fast,
she didn't have time to think about them. Then they

were collected by the folksinger whose name was John Arrowsmith. For a moment, when he came to each desk to pick up the papers, she felt him touch her and his hand was rough as sandpaper, not soft the way she imagined a musician's hand should feel, but hard like her father's.

That night Lisa did not dream. Restlessly, she tossed and turned in her sleep. When morning came, she was unwell. Her father, already out in his workshop by the time she started breakfast, was striking silver with his hammer, and the ting-tang of his hammer made her think of the folksinger named John Arrowsmith. Prickles when she thought of him. Her poem. She was afraid . . .

but was it a poem?. . . she did not know.

After breakfast, on her way to the bus stop, Lisa visited her father. He was in that meditative morning mood. Not a good time to disturb him, but she had to.

"Father, I've done a bad thing," she said.

Quickly her father's eyes met her own. Then he looked away, waiting politely for her to speak. He didn't busy himself with his jewelry this time. His hands were folded in his lap, and he waited.

"I dreamed of the turquoise horse," she said gently, "No, I dreamed not of him, I dreamed I was part of him, that I rode him all the way to the top of the sky. There I met a cloud-person who told me that the horse belonged to him. I was permitted to ride the turquoise horse, but it belonged to the family of the sun."

"You've dreamed a great dream, Lisa. You rode the turquoise horse; you've been embraced by the holy people."

He looked awed by this and she burst into tears.

He reached toward her without actually touching her, his hands outstretched, his palms open, asking.

"You don't understand," she sobbed. "Yesterday, a musician came to our class, and I liked his music. I liked him. I liked the way he played his banjo, it made everyone happy.

"This is foolish, I know. That is why I am crying. And because I think I've done a bad thing. The singer asked us to write a poem which he would put to music.

I wrote about the turquoise horse. Today, I think he will sing about it, and I am ashamed. This is like taking the silver bracelet from the spoiled grave. I had no right to tell my dream in words and put them on paper. I have stolen from a sacred grave. I am a thief."

As she said these words, her father listened without expression. When she was done, he broke into a smile.

"You have not stolen anything, child. You were given something. A blessed thing that dream was. . . but how you choose to share it is up to you—your decision, and yours alone. Remember, in the dream, the cloud-person said the horse was for all to share."

"But what if he takes my song and sells it and makes money from it. It would be a sin."

Sighing, her father said, "The world's made up of many people. Not all are righteous—but the cloud-person trusted you. . . now you must trust yourself."

That day passed slowly for Lisa. She could hear what people said to her, but they seemed to speak from such a distance, and their voices were almost inaudible. Even on the playground, shouts of her friends came to her in muffled silence. She was waiting, waiting for the moment when he would walk into the room and sing her song. She could hear his banjo ringing, his happy mustached face glowing as he sang her song. But at the same time, regardless of what her father said, she felt the awful shame of the betrayed secret. She wanted to bury her song, to hide it away forever.

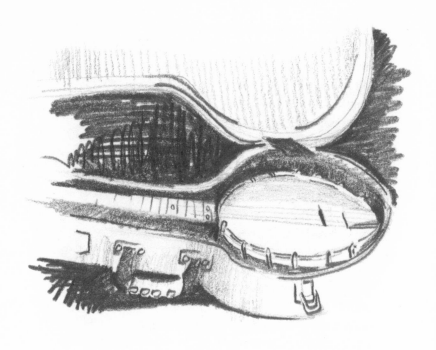

At last the moment she'd been anticipating arrived. John Arrowsmith came into the classroom. He took out his banjo and tuned it. Then he spread four pieces of art paper on a desk.

"These are your songs," he said, "and I'm going to sing them for you. Naturally, I wish I had the time to make tunes for all the things you wrote, but I only had one night...anyway, here goes..."

John Arrowsmith sang four songs, one right after

the other. The class loved them. One about a goat that butted everyone; one about a house that flew up to the moon; one with a catchy tune that went —"People these days should be nice to each other, people these days have to care for one another, people these days, people these days. . ."

Lisa didn't hear her song though. He probably hadn't even read it. The hollow feeling inside her got bigger. She was relieved because the secret of the turquoise horse was still a secret. And yet, she was disappointed. . .

After school, walking toward the bus, she saw John Arrowsmith about to get into his pickup truck. He gave her a big smile and a wave.

"You're Lisa, aren't you?"

She stopped in her tracks as he came over, his leather briefcase in hand. He had on a black cowboy hat with a horsehair hatband. Close up, he was rougher-looking than she thought. Like his hands, he was weathered in the face.

"Did I get your name right?" he asked gently.

"I'm Lisa Todachine."

"Doesn't that name mean bitterwater? If so your father's the silversmith. I'm wearing one of his buckles."

Lisa felt the warmth come around her. She liked him. She was right to have trusted him.

"He's a silversmith, while you are a poet! I didn't sing your song today because I felt it was private, something between you and your family maybe. Well, there's

another reason, too. I don't think it's really a song. There may be a fine line of difference between a song and a poem, but I think this is a poem. When you decide to really share it with people, you might think about putting it in a book."

Lisa blushed.

"Well, so long." He handed the poem back to her.

"Poem," she said to herself. What a funny word. What a funny, lovely, feeling-kind-of-word.

When she got back to her home, she put the poem of the turquoise horse on the wall of her room where anyone could see it . . . anyone in her family, that is.

But she knew, because she had changed, that her

family was growing. It now included her father and mother, her mother's family and her father's family, a cloud-person and a turquoise horse, a folksinger named John Arrowsmith, and people she had not even met who would one day read her poems in a book.

She was going to have a big family, of that she was sure.

Havasu Sam

He was sitting on a log, thinking. How long had it been? Eight years, he figured. He was 10 when it happened and now he was 18. He thought about where the years had gone, that hole in the canyon wall where spirits lived. Did they keep the years in there too? Did they keep all the ghosts and the years trapped together?

He didn't feel any older, really, or even any smarter. It was just that he had gone away from the Canyon and been educated at a private white boarding school, and there he had learned that being Indian was neither a privilege nor a problem. It was merely a fact, one he would just as soon forget about, because he would rather not be reminded of the difference. . . the color of his skin, the shape of his face, the indirect way he looked at things.

So here he was, back where he had begun. It was

not where he belonged anymore, it was where he had been, that was all. Where he had made one troublesome deep friend whom he had not been able to forget. He tasted the friend's name on his tongue: Sam. Havasu Sam, the waterfall man. He laughed to think of it. But laughter, he knew, could also bring tears—and these were tears that separated him from his old friend, Sam. As if it were only moments ago, he saw Sam move along the edge of the cliff, his fingers spread out like spiders, gripping the faulted face of stone. Barefoot, wearing nothing but his underwear. He had not forgotten, nor could he, ever. Sam was a part of him the way the fault was a part of the stone. Sam, the natural man. Sam, the breaker of rules. Sam, the hero of his childhood days.

Sam was something alright. And what was he, Jim, next to Sam? A shadow? A ghost in the Canyon wall?

Sure, he was half Havasupai. He belonged in the Canyon, the greatest canyon in the world, they said, the Grand Canyon. But, then again, his father being Navajo, he did not really belong. He was one for the open spaces, the country outside the hemmed-in walls, the horizontal land. Secretly, he loathed the poor little village where his mother's people were from, and where, every summer—June to August—he stayed, and dreamed of open space.

He saw Sam, the natural, the Havasu mentor of his childhood. The way he moved along that tricky lip of cliff-stone, all the boys waiting on the other side.

Down below was Navajo Falls, the drop several hundred feet into the bluest water in the West. And every summer the same group of boys took the same dare, crossed the cliff, went behind the falls along slippery, mossy rock, and then, where the roar of the water was not so loud, they jumped, one after the other.

He remembered it now as he sat, somewhat grown up, waiting for his old friend, Sam.

He had been terrified. Mad with fear. Trembling insane. There was no describing how much he hated heights. There was no worse thing he could think of than that crazy cascade of white water.

The others, one by one, had jumped. They had to leap out to avoid the cliff—the place where it hung out over the water like the broken wing of a wounded hawk. Not only did they have to face the fact that landing wrong could easily kill them but also there was that hawk's wing, solid rock, jagged, upon which, if they did not twist out in mid-air and make a proper jump, they would be impaled.

He remembered now just what had gone wrong inside him. How Sam, realizing that he had gotten all locked up inside, came back for him, to save him from having to go through with it. And how he had cried like a baby, just clawed into that mossy stuff with his fingers, and cried. Sam had tried, he would give him that. He'd tried to get him across, but he had failed. The long day passed and still he remained on that tricky crossing. Night came and with it, stars. The falls, loud as cannons, booming in his right ear; his body cramped and shivery. The crying over with, the other boys, including Sam, gone.

The rest he had forgotten—the precise way he got himself back on good footing, and the walk home. All that was just a blur. He had done it, simple as that. He had to, he knew it. So he had just done it. And in the dark, too.

But after that, he didn't come to the Canyon anymore. He abandoned his mother and his family. Now, after his eighteenth birthday, he had come back. He knew, no matter how well he had done in private school, there was something left unfinished that he now had to complete. So he had accepted his mother's invitation, and today, in the middle of a hot August afternoon he was waiting for his friend, the young man who was now a guide for the Canyon Campground.

Sam came up so quietly, Jim didn't hear him. The look and smell of Sam was older days, times gone by. His smile, easy and slow, came on his face and went away like smoke. Jim, on the other hand, probably smelled of the city.

They shook hands. Sam squatted on his haunches, took off the beaten straw hat he wore in hot weather, flipped it onto a willow tree. Then he tied a red bandanna around his forehead. His hair was long and blue-black in the sun.

Amazing how no words were exchanged. As Sam wiped the sweat from his eyes, Jim noticed how he had gone through the ravages of teenage acne, his face well-scarred, but especially his large fat nose. He was not handsome, but he had been a fairly good-looking boy, light-limbed and quick as a wren.

They looked at each other.

Sam smiled. "You know," he said, "nothing changes. There you are and here I am. And here's this big hunk of hole they call the Grand Canyon."

The muscles of his neck eased as Sam talked. The

voice was easy, early-old, soothing. He sounded like a wise old man, and yet he had just turned twenty.

"What's with you?" Sam asked.

"Well," he said, a little ashamedly, "private school and now, a job."

He coughed to cover his embarrassment.

Sam laughed. "Who cares?"

"You mean about school?"

"Yeah. I mean . . . If that's what you've chosen."

They looked at each other across the gulf, the canyon of years.

Sam not only sounded older, he looked a lot older.

"I made the honor roll," Jim said importantly.

Now it was Sam's turn to cough. "I buck hay and pack mules," he said, "and answer dumb tourists' questions. And the only list I ever made in school was the detention list. Don't need much education to haul gear up a hill or pack mess-kits on a mule's back."

"That's good," Jim said, nervously. What else was there to talk about, he wished he could get over this

talking part and get on with what he'd come to do.

Sam read his mind. "So you're going to have a go at it again, are you?"

There was mockery in his voice.

Jim saw himself holding on for his life. It was as if he were staring through a tube of time: here they were now, talking; there they were then, clinging.

"Can't talk you out of it?" Sam joked softly.

Jim squared his shoulders. He was taller than Sam. Superior. He kept telling himself that.

Superior.

It was simple, really. Less than fifty steps, all told.

Straight out across the lip (twenty steps); under the waterfall (ten steps); over and down to where that hawk's wing extended (twenty steps).

But halfway through the first twenty, he froze. Suppose Sam, after all these years, despised his cowardice. There was something uncertain in those glittering black eyes of his, some secret. The years were packed in them, the years that he, living elsewhere, knew nothing about. And this stopped him, caused him to break out into a fiendish sweat.

Sam, who was out in front of him, came back.

And then it was just like before—Sam, his old friend, coming back to help him, fingers outstretched like spiders.

An older memory than the falls came to him as he clung to the cliff face: he saw Sam in the catttails down below. He was showing him how to eat the soft edible salad-tasting part of the cattail. They were laughing, eating cattails. Friends.

"I can help you," Sam said. He reached out.

"Don't," he answered. "Not yet."

The fear had him. There were sharp claws in his stomach. His heart was thundering so that his chest hurt. He had his head pressed into the rock, as if it

would absorb him. Sam, next to him now, was loose, unafraid. If only, he thought, I could be like that.

"I hate school," he said loudly.

Sam said, "Easy, now. I hate it too. This is the only school there'll ever be."

"This, yes. I know. Sam, I'm scared. You don't understand about that; you're never afraid."

"Sure I am."

They were very close to each other now. They were bare-skinned and brown, both of them, though Sam was darker on the face and arms. Jim was larger and more muscular than Sam. But Sam was stronger. Fatter, maybe. But stronger. His legs were like fence posts.

The spray from the falls was washing their faces in the wind. He was shivering.

Sam, the water beads rolling off his cheeks, said,

"I've been scared before. Dead scared. So I know."

Jim talked into the rock, his fingers stuck in the cracks. If I fall, he thought, it will be minus my fingers. "Sam, you don't know, you can't."

"I know." The water was coming off his face in ribbons. That rough and ragged face was older than its years.

"What do you know?" He couldn't talk any more. He needed everything now, even his breath, to hold on.

"I'm scared," Sam said dryly. "Every time I leave our people I'm scared."

"But you don't know because you're not afraid to die."

"No, but I'm afraid. Afraid of the world outside. Sam, the waterfall man — afraid to live."

Jim looked sharply to his right to see Sam's face. The sudden movement made him lose his grip in his right hand. Sam flicked his left hand like a rattlesnake.

"I gotcha, Buddy, I gotcha."

It was the old name. Sam called him Buddy. Like he used to. That made him want to laugh.

"Sam, I want to laugh."

"You do what you want, Buddy. But no matter what you do, just remember I gotcha."

He laughed then. It came out in a sudden quick volley of harsh gasps. Then it was over.

"Why didn't you grab me. . .way back; how come you. . .left me, Sam?"

Sam hooted so loud in his ear, the falls got quiet. But still, the rattler-hand was dug in deep, and Sam's body didn't shake when he laughed, the laughter just spilled out into the sun.

"I never left you, Buddy."

"You were there?"

"I was there the whole time. Crouched under that tree, right there, with my rope. I had a big loop built up. No way was I going to let Buddy slip off. No way."

"I've been a fool."

"We're all fools. Now and again. I been one myself . . .can't remember when but—"

"Do you know there's no word in Navajo for 'I love you.' "

Sam didn't say anything. The water was on his lower lip. He blew it off and looked away.

Buddy went on, "There's *ayò anoshnì*, and that word means. . .Well, it kind of means, I like you a lot, I like you more than most things put together, I like you enough to walk under these falls and get the heck out of here—"

"Aw," Sam said, "I was hopin' you were going to give me a little peck on the cheek."

They both laughed again and started to move along the lip of rock.

The rest was fire and smoke, moss and rock. They inched along the lip until they were under the spume of the waterfall. There it was slick, Sam had said, "as deer guts." They got out from under it alright, and then there was the slight descent, the curve of fire, the boys called it, because the rock on that part physically burned the soles of the feet.

Sam told him not to look. Whatever you do, Sam said, keep your eyes on your hands, on where you put your hands on the rock. Think of nothing but hands on rock. Then, turn, suddenly, and jump out as far as your body will let you go. Over the hawk's wing, and down— the bad part over, the worst part begun. Let yourself go, he said, let yourself fall, let your bones go soft. Drop like a baby bird, straight down.

And Buddy plummeted into the redeeming waters below.

Running
Girl

T here was Gila Monster, wrinkled and old. Sometimes Running Girl thought he looked like a man.
Sometimes not. He was old though, that was for sure,
and his voice sounded like sandpaper.

"Don't run," he said, "don't run if you don't want to."

His right forefoot trembled a little when he spoke,
and his eyes were dark as day old blood.

Running Girl was only sixteen. Fast and bright,
quick as anything. She could run for hours when she felt
like it. The trouble was she didn't know if she felt like it
now. For one thing, this place where she was staying
made her feel funny. Second Mesa, Hopi country. All
these quietly moving, partly smiling people. They weren't
her people, they weren't Navajo. Something was easy in
them. Navajos were not easy. If anything they were
hard—even she, being Navajo, knew the hardness that

an outsider might see or feel. Navajos pushed where
Hopis put themselves away from pushing. She resented
Hopis always saying they were the first people. And
believing it. They smiled pretty enough. They ran okay.
They were people. But they weren't dineh, they weren't
The People, they weren't her people.

And here she was sitting up in bed in the early hours
of the morning, talking about all this with a gila monster
and a hummingbird. Talking about whether she would
run or not. In a few hours, Sun Father would touch the
houses of the Hopi. She shook her head. This place
where she was staying, its door didn't face east, if she was
not careful she would miss Sun Father's first rays of light.

Hummingbird came forward now and said something in Running Girl's ear. He had the voice of cornhusks. Dry, dry.

"When I was elected as First Healer, all the other birds were jealous."

She liked Hummingbird especially because his heart was honey, he had sun inside him, and he spoke in a tiny voice that was made of dry pods.

She laughed at his head, which was so much rounder than hers, so perfectly round like the little wonder of an egg he made.

"Blackbird, yellowbird and warbler all were jealous. But they knew that though I was small, I was also wise.

I showed them how to hold the sacred red flower and how to sing into the sunrise. . . now they always listen when I come around."

Running Girl touched the top of Hummingbird's round, green-gold, lavender head, and said, "At break of day, I always hear bird people singing their good medicine songs—"

"—The songs I taught them," Hummingbird said.

"But how am I to teach my people, if I don't even know if I want to run. . . today is the big race, and I don't know."

Gila Monster's left forefoot gave a little shake and he shuddered slightly. "I must go," he said.

"—But—"

And he limped off into the coming dawn.

Hummingbird—his wings never still—whirred very close to her ear. She listened to his wings make the

sound of small bells in the cornrows. Then he faded into the deep gloom of her room in the Hopi Cultural Center. She was left, sitting there in her nightdress, in a pile of tangled sheets wondering if she was dreaming.

The time had come. She walked to the hotel window that faced east and opened it. A draft of icy air came into the room and ruffled the curtains, as well as her long straight black hair.

She stood there feeling cold in her cotton nightdress, saying the morning prayer. Then she pinched some cornmeal from the paper sack she kept in her pocketbook and sprinkled the four directions. The little flecks of yellow meal seemed to glow upon the dark brown carpeting of the Hopi hotel. Then she got back into bed, and with the window wide open and smelling of dawn, she closed her eyes for a brief second and fell asleep.

Running Girl dreamed then that she was running a

race long, long ago. She was leading by many yards. Her
feet, which were bare, touched the sand so slightly, she
believed she must be running on water. Behind her,
however, she heard the footfalls of more than a hundred
runners.

She had no problem with her breathing. The air
that she needed to breathe was not outside but inside
her. When she had too much of it, she let it out, like a
peaceful sigh.

She awoke. It was almost six a.m., time to dress for the race. Without a trace of doubt, she prepared to run.

That morning passed quickly for Running Girl. She ran in the junior division and won a 5,000 kilometer victory over 32 young women from tribes all over the Southwest. She ran barefoot over the frozen sands of Hopi, facing the golden sunlit village of Shipaulovi as she poured on her greatest strength.

She won. But that was not what made her glad. The sand underfoot felt like water. Her breathing was effortless. And though the race was long and hard and the winter air cold, she heard a hummingbird singing behind her ear.

* * * *

One week later Running Girl was at the TAC National Cross Country Championships in Raleigh, North Carolina. It was a strange damp hardwood country she found herself running in this time, going along a course that wound snakelike through oaks and briars, pastel fields and dirty-smelling ponds full of dark leaves. The girls who ran trials with her were lanky creatures who seemed ideally built for cruising the hills. Girls designed for sprinting, it appeared, forever.

Running Girl compared herself to them and came out, in her own judgment, poorly. She was short and compactly built, with legs for the long uphill haul over mesa tops scattered with loose rocks. She was small in size next to these magnified white-skinned people who

wore their hair close against bone-sharp faces. These were lean people who looked like they never lost.

That first day of trials her thigh started to trouble her. Sparks traveled up from her knee and burned at her hip. She ran with a noticeable limp, and her coach told her to take it easy for the day, knock off and go back to her room and rest.

Lying on top of the bed at the expensive hotel that was even more foreign to her than the hotel at Hopi, she thought of the four directions. She had forgotten to bring cornmeal along with her. She hadn't risen with the Sun Father. She'd slept fitfully, not well.

Was there a blessing for those who forgot to be blessed? She didn't know what it was, but there had to be one. The Blessing Way, of course. How could she have forgotten? It covered all kinds of offenses to the Holy People. Why was she having a hard time remembering who she was and where she had come from? Was it because she didn't like the way she was—her dark skin, her long hair, her small strong body?

She had seen gods, it was true. They were white. They talked in silly, breathy voices about nothing. But they wore gleaming suits of skin-tight uniform, and they had vacant eyes and trim legs and no hips to speak of, and they talked, talked, talked—and she couldn't, Running Girl couldn't even draw a breath in their presence. They were bright cold flames that you touch and are burnt by. So she said nothing to them. And they said nothing to her.

But in the night a hot wet wind came up out of the woods. It smelled sweetly of dying flowers, and Running Girl was instinctively afraid of it because she knew that there are good winds and bad, and this one was bad. The way it kept coming and coming, never stopping—and the way the blackbirds in the leafless oak trees shrilled against it, rising in mad circles, spinning off in

a southerly direction. Running Girl was afraid.

The hot wet wind came from the north. The black-birds shouted at it, and this doing no good, left in heaving swarms and were heard no more. Then it was only this wind with its pressure of dying flowers, snuffling all around her room. She closed the patio door. But the wind, after she'd gotten into bed, kept snouting against the door.

Sleep did not come easily. When it finally took her, she saw bright crooked flashes of lightning. Waking up, she stared out the glass patio door. A plastic lawn chair was crawling along on its side, in pain. Oak leaves were pasted to the glass. The hot dead wind was in the room. It had come through the ventilators. Outside winter thunder rumbled like a bad stomach. And whenever she closed her eyes, she saw the cracked forks of lightning. But only when she closed them. When they were open, the night roared blank and dark.

"I am safe," Running Girl said aloud to the empty room, "I am safe in my house of pollens. Whatever you do," she said to the wind, "you cannot take that away. For I choose to run in beauty, beauty will be around me. And though you will attack the door of my sacred house, I will not let you in."

Running Girl knew this sounded like the Big Bad Wolf, but in her mind wolves traveled at night on two legs and tore throats and drank blood. And winds, like two-legged wolves, were capable of killing. And she had believed pollens would do no good in such a strange purple place as North Carolina.

In the morning it was on the news. A tornado had cut a fat swath of darkness across the land while she slept. It had torn a shopping center to sticks and killed 11 people and injured more than a hundred. The tornado had come so close to the hotel, she had heard it carving wood like a drunken power saw, chewing it and spitting it, so that splinters pinged against the double glass door.

At dawn, though there was no sun and no direction she could call east, she closed her eyes as she had the night before, and envisioned the house of pollen with its doorway opening for the Sun Father. Stepping through the door into the new day, she knew that He was with her.

The 5,000 kilometer course through the hazy hardwood forest of maples and poplars was untouched by the storm. Every tree stood as it had the night before. Every branch dripped with rain and the oak-leaved paths were slick. Helicopters hovered near, rescuing the stranded and injured, but the race, the national finals cross country race, was on.

* * * *

On the jet going home, she remembered the twists where she fell and the turns where she braked into the pain of her sore hip. The changing of gears, the grinding coming-up off the hills, the long straight stretch of the flat marsh-soaked meadows. Out of 25 girls, ranging in age from 14 to 18 she had finished 10th. She was, therefore, the 10th best cross country junior division athlete in the nation. The fact that it meant nothing to her, nothing at all, was tinged with the knowledge that her prayer, late and full of fear, had protected her. And now she was in an airplane, flying at 30,000 feet, preparing to eat an airtight bag of salted nuts.

The shiny silver medal she had won was in her palm, so she gave it to the man next to her. He tucked up his newspaper, and not knowing what else to say, said, "Well, well, what have we here?"

Jimmy Blue Eyes

Like wolves pawing in the dirt, the children of Jemez Pueblo drew into a dense pack and prepared to run.

Some yards away, squatting under a big ponderosa, was an old man with shoulder-length hair the color of snow. Beside him stood his grandson, an eight-year-old named Jimmy Blue Eyes, whose namesake eyes were a shocking shade of blue against his dark skin.

"You can win this race, Jimmy," his grandfather said, "but you must remember what I've taught you."

Jimmy was listening, but his eyes were fixed on the black obsidian bear worn on a rawhide thong around his grandfather's neck. The bear, like the boy, had bright blue turquoise eyes.

"Are you listening to me, Jimmy?"

"You want me to do what you've taught me to do."

"And what is that, Jimmy?"

"To run without thinking about running . . . to run like the wind . . . to just run!"

The old man whose name was Ray Joe chuckled softly.

"That is right," he said. "Now remember the story I told you—"

"—The one about the bear. . ."

Jimmy again became lost in the magnified image of the obsidian bear worn by his grandfather; it seemed to grow in size as he looked at it, and then to shrink back.

"Remember, once you have touched a bear while you are running, you will always have his power— unless he comes after you and takes it back."

"What happens then, Granpa?"

"Then the bear kills you and takes back his medicine."

While Jimmy and his grandfather, Ray Joe, talked softly in the shadow of the ponderosa, the other runners waited in anticipation. They were lined up now in a ragged formation three bodies deep, fifteen in all, and most of them a good head taller than Jimmy.

Ray Joe got to his feet and held up an eagle feather between his fingers.

"When this touches the earth, you start," he said.

The boys looked eagerly at the feather, and Jimmy found his place at the back of the pack.

The feather was held out at arm's length. Every boy's eye was trained on it as it was released, falling almost in slow motion, a melodic arcing motion, quill over

end, lightly touching the earth. Instantly, the runners broke from their trance. The uphill trail, a winding grade through splintery sunlight and pine shadow, was suddenly choked with dust.

Jimmy was last to disappear over the dust-clouded ridge.

Not far from where the boys ran, a herd of elk listened with pricked ears and wet sensitive noses. They somehow knew that it was a race, for hunters did not travel in such numbers. But a squirrel, chittering angrily from a pine bough, did not know this and continued to scold long after all but Jimmy Blue Eyes had passed its tree.

Jimmy was still trying to catch up with the others when he came down the slope that led to a deep sandy arroyo. Behind the arroyo toward the east was a small meadow where a mother bear and her two cubs were foraging for grubs in a lightning-struck log. When the boys burst into the arroyo in a great wave of thudding feet, the mother bear woofed loudly, wheeled around in a westerly direction, and herded her cubs along with her. But one of the cubs lost step, and confused by the sudden clamor, took off in the wrong direction. This cub, bawling loudly as it ran, forefeet touching hindfeet, tum-

bled into the arroyo and collided with Jimmy Blue Eyes.

For a moment the boy, and the bear both toppled head over heels and lay still in the sand, their eyes glued to each other. Then the little cub who had never seen a boy before touched its nose to Jimmy's, and each of them jumped up and resumed their own personal race in opposite directions.

From under the ponderosa where he sat with his back to the bark, Ray Joe heard what sounded to him

like a war whoop. He was certain it came from his grandson, and he smiled because deep in his bones, he knew what that meant.

* * * *

Five years later, Jimmy Blue Eyes, age 14, was one of the best runners at Jemez Pueblo. Whenever there was a community run of any kind, Jimmy participated, even though he was already a varsity athlete with a State medal to his credit.

Each spring on the morning that Ray Joe had announced for the race, the same familiar group of boys gathered together on a hill a couple miles from the Pueblo and ran as friends, fellow students, and members of the ancient brotherhood of the Pueblo.

This spring was no exception; the boys, as usual, were lined up like wolves, but this time Ray Joe was not there... something had kept him from his duty as feather-dropper. However, Jimmy was prepared to take his place, and holding the feather aloft as his grandfather had always done, he let it go. Before it even touched the ground Jimmy was meshed in with the other runners. Around his neck was the sacred black bear given him by Ray Joe; it was his now, and everyone knew the story and the power of the bear that came from Jimmy when he ran.

Up the torturous slope they went, through the arroyo, and up into the pine trees where the generations of squirrels held their noisy quarters. Jimmy moved with ease, his hands almost touching his hips, his body bent slightly forward, his knees crouched, his feet falling flat and smooth as he took the turns, passing runner after runner, moving far ahead of the pack.

Down in the adobe village where Jimmy's family lived, Ray Joe looked up from the corral where he was working with a young spunky appaloosa mare named Canela. He knew the boys were running. He knew his place was with them—why had this foolish filly caused him such a morning of grief? He had hoped to ride up on the hill, confidently straddling this horse "that couldn't be broke."

But it hadn't worked that way, and now he was still trying to mount the stubborn animal whose head kept jerking at its hackamore, whinnying and snorting.

"Now don't take it out on me," the old man said under his breath as he eased himself onto the filly's bare back. "Just let me . . ."

But the appaloosa danced backward in the corral and reared high into the air, and Ray Joe, hanging on desperately to the rope hackamore, dropped from her back and fell under her hooves.

From where he ran, the leader of the race by many yards, Jimmy suddenly caught the worst cramp he had ever known. It hit him like a hammer, clenching his right calf with such agony that he lost a step, tripped and landed, face-first, in the dirt.

Jimmy came limping into the yard in time to see the

ambulance leave with his grandfather.

He hobbled painfully into the kitchen where his mother and father were drinking coffee. The look in their eyes told him that what had happened was serious.

"How bad is he?" Jimmy asked his mother, who shook her head, indicating she did not want to talk at that moment.

Jimmy looked at his father. There was this difference between them: Jimmy's father was born and raised at Jemez; his mother, Ray Joe's daughter, was Navajo. In the Navajo way, custom dictated that the mother of the family was head of the household. Jimmy saw his mother's control over this situation, and he wondered what it might mean.

"Just tell me how he is," Jimmy said.

"Not good," his father answered. "He has fractured his collarbone, cracked three of his ribs and dislocated his hip. You know how old he is, ninety-four, older maybe. He was unconscious after Canela threw him."

Jimmy's mother said, "I think that he will want to die. No one that old can survive such an injury—he also took a blow to the head, one of Canela's hooves..."

"How can you talk of death?" Jimmy said. "What do we know standing here, talking? We should be at the hospital with Granpa, helping him."

Jimmy's father, whose name was Tomas, gave a loud sigh and sat down in one of the kitchen chairs. It was a long narrow room set off from the rest of the

65

house because it had been built much earlier, probably in the eighteenth century sometime. The walls were cracked adobe, the floor cracked linoleum; the kitchen sink had a standing pipe with a long arched handle for pumping water. Most of the room was taken up by an old porcelain woodburner. The table where the family ate was directly in front of this stove.

Tomas said, "It's time you faced some things, Jimmy. Death is one of them. Back when I was a kid, some of the old people used to die in the old way by just closing their eyes. But changing times made hospitals the place to go to do that. Your mother's people see it this way: When an old one is going out of this world, the white man's hospital is almost like a mortuary."

"Tomas," Jimmy's mother, Emma, said: "You make it sound so cold, so antiseptic. Our people have used the hospitals as you say, but only when it was known that someone was going to die. This is up to Granpa, we don't know that—"

"I'm not going to let him die!" Jimmy announced, his eyes streaked with tears.

"It's not up to us," Tomas said, "it's up to him."

"Do either of you know how old he really is?" Emma asked.

"You stupid horse," Jimmy yelled at the back window, "I hate you!"

"It wasn't Canela, Jimmy—you know it wasn't," Emma said.

"It's my fault, I should've been here helping him. It's just not fair!" He looked at his father with a blank expression.

"I have to go to work," Tomas explained as he left the room.

Jimmy looked at his mother whose face was clear, untroubled.

" How can you be so, so—" Jimmy tightened his lips into a line.

She said, "So calm?"

"Yes, and at a time like this—he's your father!"

"Jimmy, Granpa is going to die. I saw it in his face when he was lying in the corral. Do you know about the Dead, Jimmy? Have I ever told you that they come back? We—our people—believe there are certain precautions that must be taken so that the Dead can't come back and hurt the living. We believe in the old ways. You take a sick person to the white hospital to die so that the dying person's spirit can't come back. The ghost won't return, or if it does, it goes back to the last place it rested, the hospital. That's why we are not going to see your grandpa. He will go out of this world, alone."

Jimmy looked at his mother with scorn.

"That's junk—bunch of superstitious junk. Mom, you're crazy!" He glanced at her sideways, wondering how she would react, a little worried at what he had just said.

Emma crossed the room swiftly, took hold of his shoulders and shook them roughly.

"You'll do as I say, Jimmy." Her face showed more than a trace of anger.

The middle of that same day at Holy Cross Hospital, two nurses were folding down a bedsheet to restrain Jimmy's grandfather, Ray Joe, who, although still half-unconcious, was thrashing from side to side, trying to sit up.

"You know, Beverly," the head nurse said, "this might be too tight. . ." She was an older woman with

bluish hair, heavily rouged cheeks, which darkened the shadows around her eyes.

"It'll hold him, Lyn, you can be sure of it," the other woman said, smiling pertly, tucking in the sheet.

Ray Joe muttered some words in Navajo. His long white hair spread out on the pillowcase gave his dark face the frozen wooden look of a death mask.

"Wonder what he's saying..." said Lyn, moving toward the door.

Then Ray Joe said these words clearly in English: "Jimmy, Jimmy Blue Eyes...where are you, Jimmy Blue Eyes?"

"With these old ones," Beverly said, "it breaks your heart." She smiled wanly, her hand replacing a curl that was out of place. "After all these years, I don't think I'm the least bit wiser. I've seen a lot of Indians come and go, and it gets to you. It really does. You take this one here, Lyn, he's all by himself, and he'll go out that way, too. Poor old man. Poor us, too."

"Why do you say 'poor us'?" Lyn asked in surprise.

"Because we're the ones who have to be here all the time dealing with it. If this old man's family stays true to form, they'll let him pass on all by himself. It wasn't always that way; you see in the days of the medicine men, everyone got healed in the traditional way—the sandpainting, the sing, the family present, everyone a part of it. But in these forgetful times of ours when there's no medicine men anymore, and no earthly modern

70

medicine to bring him out of it, well, it's awfully sad."

She breathed a sigh and shook her head. "I heard another story about why the family doesn't come around," Lyn said.

"Oh, you mean the bother about the ghost," Beverly interrupted, "I've heard that one a thousand times, if I've heard it once. Navajos will tell you—and I mean perfectly straightforward—that ghosts will come back and haunt people. They'll let us handle the body after it's gone on, they'll act like it was never here. Then they'll burn the hogan where the dying person lay, just to get rid of the past."

71

"The past?" Lyn questioned, glancing at Ray Joe's bed with concern.

"You know, the evidence of the dead person's having been there, they dispose of everything that would lead the ghost back to its final resting place."

"Kinda spooky, if you ask me."

"Now look at that face, will you? That's a face you're not likely to forget. I'll bet he's over a hundred...could be he saw the last of the Indian Wars—"

"Could be he was in one himself," Lyn chuckled.

* * * *

It was late afternoon with the afterglow on the hills when Jimmy got back from track practice. His mother was in the kitchen cutting up chunks of potato for some chili stew. Jimmy came in quietly through the back door and his mother greeted him.

"Have a good practice?" she asked, turning again to the potatoes.

"Lousy."

"Why do you say that, Jimmy?"

"Do you really need to ask?" he said miserably.

Emma faced her son: "The nurse said his condition's stable."

"What's that supposed to mean?"

"Stable," Emma said, "means no worse."

"You said he was going to die."

"It's up to him."

"But it's up to you whether I go visit him or not,"

Jimmy said sarcastically, his voice rising.

"There are some things you don't understand—yet," Emma said softly. Her face was gentle, kind.

"You're right, I don't," Jimmy snapped, "and the reason is that I don't want to. Granpa ought to go to the hospital to get better, not to die by himself."

"He's not alone, Jimmy. The nurse—"

"I don't want to hear about it."

"Jimmy, do you know who you're talking to?" Emma's face was firm with resolve.

"My mother." he said blankly.

Emma dropped the sharp knife and the potato she was carving and came to the chair where Jimmy slouched, chin on chest, blowing air into his shirt.

"When my mother, your grandmother," Emma said, "died on the reservation, we knew when she was on her deathbed. Your grandfather knew it, I knew it, and so did everybody else in the family. Your grandfather took her to the white hospital in Gallup. He left her there and she died. That was the way it was."

Without looking up, Jimmy said, "It sounds like the way the Eskimos used to put their old people out to die on a chunk of ice. I always thought that tribe was really primitive. You know, old-time savage types. Maybe that's why this thing gets me the way it does. Like, the hospital's one big ice flow or something."

Emma's face warmed in the red light coming in the window.

"Do you mean to say that you're afraid we're—your father and I—acting . . . how did you put it? . . . savage, or something?"

Jimmy slunk deeper into the straight-backed chair, his eyes staring at his silver concho buckle.

"Yeah, that's how I see it," he slurred.

"Do you know the Navajo story of the First World?" Emma asked.

"They come out of the earth like ants—I don't remember, I heard it a long time ago."

"Long ago," Emma began, and her voice had a certain music in it, "before anything was much of anything, there was a beginning. And in this beginning, there was a cave that went deep into the earth, and the animal people and the two-leggeds came out of this cave. But on the fourth day, one of the animal people got lost . . . I think it was a chief's daughter—"

"—You said animal people—"

"They have chiefs, too, Jimmy. Anyway, where was I? Oh, yes, the animal chiefs . . . now I remember, they went back with some two-leggeds—"

"Are the two-leggeds us?"

"Yes, now stop interrupting. They looked into the cave of the underworld where life began and when they looked down into it, they died."

"What for?"

"That is what I'm trying to tell you. It is not for us to see. That world is closed to us. Unless, of course, we are dying. Then that is where we go."

"Back to where it all began, I get it. It's awfully primitive, mom, I hate to tell you—"

"But you do," Emma said, hopefully, ". . .understand. . ."

"Yeah, I get it. It does kinda make sense, I guess."

"Of course it makes sense. Jimmy, this is your religion."

"Maybe. If I want it to be," he said uncertainly.

Then he got up and left the kitchen.

Before dinner Jimmy lay on his bed, thinking. It had been a hard practice and he was tired. Closing his eyes for a moment, he fell into a deep dreamless sleep. Then he woke into a dream.

In the dream he saw Ray Joe walking on a long dark road. The road led to a great hole in the ground. His grandfather was nearing that hole.

"Come back, Grandfather," Jimmy called.

Slowly, Ray Joe turned to his grandson. Then Jimmy saw that his grandfather's face was made of darkness.

"Come back," Jimmy called again, but his voice was so small it sounded like a tiny bird.

"Such a long way back, I'm almost home now."

"No," Jimmy cried, "Come back with me, I'll take care of you."

"Long way back. . ." Ray Joe said from far, far away.

Jimmy woke up in a film of sweat, his heart pounding as if he'd been on the track at school. Where am I?

he wondered. Then he understood that it had been a dream...but so real. He had never experienced a dream like that one.

At dinner his parents talked about Ray Joe. They spoke of the good things he had done in his life. His father told the story of how Ray Joe had been one of the trackers hired by the U.S. government to chase after Geronimo. He and his men had run for three days and three nights. They ran all the way to Mexico after

Geronimo, and they finally caught him. And that was the last war, the last Indian war.

And his mother told of the time Ray Joe tracked the bear until he was able to reach out and touch it. He had gone to Black Mountain looking for Bear and he'd found him and tagged him, and then brother Bear decided to tag him, and Ray Joe had had to run another mile before Bear gave up and shambled back to Black Mountain. Jimmy learned that Ray Joe had been clawed that time, and he had dripped blood all the way home.

But the image that stayed in Jimmy's mind all during dinner was the face of his grandfather in the dream. The face made of darkness.

That evening as he prepared to do his homework, Jimmy decided on a plan. It was simple. All he had to do was go outside and feed Canela, and instead of coming inside and finishing up his homework, he would head over the hill to the hospital.

* * * *

Jimmy walked down the long, bright, unfriendly corridor. At each door he stopped and peeked into the room. Then he backed out, checking and rechecking the room number on the door before moving on. The place was unfamiliar to him—the lights too bright, the odorless smell of cleanliness. And there was the danger of nurse-movements, the stiff briskness, a formality that frightened him. He was not used to such places. It was the first hospital he had ever been in.

But down at the end of the third floor convalescent corridor, Jimmy found what he was looking for; he ducked into the room quickly, as if its semidarkness would hide him from the hall and the patrol of white-uniformed nurses.

There was his grandfather, Ray Joe, snowy hair spread out on his pillow, in a half-raised position on the adjustable bed.

Jimmy coughed nervously to let his grandfather know he was entering the room. The old man's eyes fluttered opened, a faint smile spreading across his lips.

"Who is it?" Ray Joe said hoarsely.

"Me. Jimmy."

"Jimmy, Jimmy. Come over to me."

He walked to the bed, glanced disapprovingly at the restraining sheet tucked across his grandfather's hips.

"What's this thing doing here?" Jimmy hissed.

"That's my hackamore tie-down. Kind of keeps me in line."

"You can't hardly move, Granpa...who put this here?" Jimmy demanded.

"The ladies in white, I guess. Don't be too hard on them, Jimmy, they think they're trying to help this old man get well. I heard I was thrashing around like that filly of yours."

Jimmy put his hand on his grandfather's shoulder.

"You promised me," he said, "you wouldn't ride Canela until she was ready."

Ray Joe looked sheepishly at his grandson.

"She was ready, I wasn't. But didn't you make a promise to your mother?"

"What one?"

"The one about not coming to the hospital." He winked.

Jimmy looked away, staring out the window at the rising moon coming off the sand hills by the hospital parking lot.

"Can I make you more comfortable, Granpa?"

"There's no comfort in dying, Jimmy. Besides, you don't expect me to lie back against this pillow, do you?"

"Why not?" Jimmy asked, pinching the pillow that was propped up behind his grandfather.

"It's stuffed full of feathers, that's why."

Ray Joe stared peevishly at Jimmy. He could not believe his grandson didn't know about such things.

Jimmy stared at the rising moon.

"There's much you don't know about being Navajo, Jimmy. Take this pillow away from me because if I sleep on it, I'll wake up in the morning with feathers growing out of my neck. I had bad dreams on account of this pillow, and now I'm going to have a chicken neck."

Their conversation was interrupted by the night nurse passing by on her rounds. A brisk middle-aged woman with red hair came to the bed to check Ray Joe's pulse. The sharp smell of perfume confused the air around the bed.

"So Grandfather has a visitor," she said dreamily, tucking the sheet in.

Ray Joe didn't answer; he looked at the nurse emptily. Jimmy saw the light in his face come and go.

"How are we doing this evening?" the nurse said cheerily filling a paper cup with fresh water.

"Me or the boy?" Ray Joe asked.

"Well, let's see, shall I examine the young one, too?" the nurse said, trying to keep the conversation alive.

Shrinking away from the bed, Jimmy Blue Eyes took a seat in one of the chairs by the wall.

Ray Joe smiled. "It's the boy's fault I'm here. He made me get on this wild horse of his. The horse threw me for a loop and that's how I got tied up in a bedsheet at Holy Cross Hospital."

"On a horse—at your age!" she said stiffly.

From across the dark room, Jimmy smirked, "He breaks them for a living."

"Not for a living, Jimmy, I do it for the hell of it," Ray Joe said, the light returning to his eyes.

The nurse placed her hands on her hips and pursed her lips thoughtfully.

"I don't think you do it for the hell of it," she said, "I think you catch hell for doing it!"

"The only old horse got broke this time was me," Ray Joe muttered, his eyes glittering.

Having placed a thermometer in the corner of Ray Joe's mouth while they were talking, she now examined it under the table light by the bed.

"Well, here's another thing that just broke—your fever."

"Can I loosen these sheets?" Jimmy asked the nurse now that she had shown them her sense of humor.

"You better not. They're for his own good. Why, he's been thrashing around ever since he got here. Well, I'm on my way out. . .call if you need me. . ." But she didn't finish her sentence. She left the room more suddenly than she'd entered it.

"The care you get here, Jimmy," Ray Joe said after she had gone, "it's not care, really, it's just careful. Back in the old days a singer would sing you back to health, and he knew just how to do it."

Jimmy edged closer to the bed. He watched the glow come to his grandfather's face again. He saw it turn familiar, the face of a man who had once tagged a bear and run after Geronimo.

"What was it like, Granpa?"

"You mean the old sings? Well, they were. . ." and his eyes clouded with memory and brightened in the hollow sockets of his dark face.

"When I was a boy long ago, a singer came to our hogan and he made a dry painting on the sand floor, and he had me sit on it. Then he started to sing, and you know, Jimmy, even after all these years, I can still

remember his words."

"How long ago was it?"

"Ninety years," he said in a hushed voice.

"And can you still sing that song?"

Ray Joe began to chant softly under his breath. "These are your hands, your friends—" he said in Navajo. "These are your feet, your friends...These are your ribs, your friends...These are your—" he broke off, tired, out of breath.

"The singer's song made you well?" Jimmy asked.

"Not only the singer, Jimmy. The dry painting I sat on was for the holy people to come join me. When the singer finished his song, he asked me to step away from that painting. Then my family stepped into it and they walked with the holy people. That was how I was cured."

"I wish," Jimmy said regretfully, "we had that singer here now."

Ray Joe smiled and the light faded from his eyes. "I'm so tired, Jimmy...so very tired."

"I called to you in my dream," Jimmy said.

"Yes, you did. You called me back. And I am here now. But soon I will go again."

Jimmy touched his grandfather's hand.

"Don't go yet," he said quietly, "there are things I don't understand."

"What things, Jimmy?"

Jimmy drew near to his grandfather's face and whispered, "I don't understand... about ghosts...why they come back. . ."

"There is a place to the north," Ray Joe told him, "a hole in the earth, and when you get there, the members of your family who have gone on before you, they come. They are the guardians, and they test you to make sure you are one of them."

Jimmy squeezed his grandfather's hand again.

"Do you have to go there, Granpa?"

"My family is waiting for me, I saw them at the entrance of that hole."

"Your family is here, Granpa, waiting for you right now." Tears suddenly filled Jimmy's eyes and he began to cry.

"You asked about ghosts," Ray Joe said, "we believe in them, Jimmy. We believe they can return and do harm."

"You're my friend, you wouldn't hurt me Granpa."

"We don't know what I'd do. . .only those who die before uttering a cry into this world, infants and old people. . .only those pass into the shadow place without coming back."

Jimmy tried to see through his tears, but the face of his grandfather was as dim as his dream.

"Granpa, if you were to die, here, in this hospital, you'd die of old age. You wouldn't come back."

Ray Joe shook his head meaningfully. "The night before I was thrown by Canela," he said, "I had a dream, and in this dream I saw Canela dying. I should have

known it was me and not the horse. There are things a man knows, Navajo things. Old ways. We say when a man counts his days, he will know them by heart. One day this will kill him. It is best not to know your age. No, Jimmy, if I die here, it wouldn't be because of old age. But because I am a stubborn man who doesn't listen to his dreams. I deserve to die. Now. . .you must let me rest, Jimmy Blue Eyes."

"I won't," Jimmy said angrily, "I won't."

Ray Joe seemed amused. "You won't?" he said, "why not?"

"Because you said your ghost, your shadow, might come back. Now I know how to keep that from happening."

"You do?" Surprised, Ray Joe continued to stare at Jimmy. The boy, just then, had sounded so much like a man, it made Ray Joe remember his own mind, how at fourteen he had changed, how it had happened all in one day, the day of the bear.

Jimmy worked his fingers under the mattress. He pulled at the sheet the nurses had tucked in.

"You don't know what you're doing," Ray Joe said sharply.

"I do, Granpa. I know how to run a race."

"What does a race have to do with dying in a hospital?"

"When you ran after Geronimo," Jimmy said, jerking out the bedsheet on the opposite side of the bed, "you ran until you caught up with him. You didn't quit. You kept running. And that's what you've taught me to do. Tonight, we run together."

"Who are we running after this time?" Ray Joe chuckled.

"We're running after your shadow."

"We never did catch Geronimo," Ray Joe mused, "never laid eyes on the man. Well, that story's all balled up."

Jimmy stopped pulling blankets from his grandfather's bed. "The story's all a lie?" he said as if betrayed.

"The old runner, Geronimo, died with a smile on his lips—and you know why?—because he'd outwitted his captors. They got him, his body, but they never got his spirit. He died in the year nineteen hundred and nine; I was born in the year eighteen hundred and eighty-six."

"You still could've run after him."

"Could've doesn't mean did. You ever hear of a newborn baby running across the desert? Now that would make some news worth reading!"

"Granpa, if you know the day you were born, you know how old you are. And if you know how old you are, that's bad luck. You said, 'If a man counts his days—' "

"—So who's counting? Hey, I thought you were going to help me get out of this bed?"

Jimmy did not stop to see the light come back into his grandfather's eyes. He went across the room and got the chrome wheelchair folded against the wall.

"Here, Granpa," he said, "we've got a race to run."

A few minutes later the night nurse, who saw the dark boy and his white-haired grandfather heading down the hall did a double-take. First, she smiled sweetly as Jimmy wheeled by her, nonchalant as any Sunday visitor. Then her smile withered and her mouth dropped open. She didn't need to look at the clock to know that it was past visiting hours, but she looked anyway, and then, the boy and the old man, much to her amazement, were heading for the elevator. It was then the impossible thought occurred to her: the two of them were leaving the hospital!

"Jimmy, Jimmy Blue Eyes," Ray Joe sang as they waited for the elevator doors to open. Then, "Did I ever tell you how you got that name?"

"Some other time, Granpa," Jimmy said. A look of alarm had come over his face as he watched the procession of nurses coming their way.

"I hope this elevator isn't stuck between floors," he said.

Then the doors made a sucking sound and gasped open. An old woman in a housecoat was inside the elevator. A girl Jimmy's age was standing next to her.

"Is this Four?" the old woman croaked, "We're on our way up to Four."

"We're heading down to One," Ray Joe snorted, "then we're going on the big run home."

"Oh, they've released you, how wonderful!" the old woman wheezed.

"Let us in," Jimmy urged.

The old woman placed her right hand on the girl's shoulder. "Lead the way, dear," she sighed. Jimmy wheeled Ray Joe into the empty elevator.

The old woman turned around, and the nurses who just then had caught up with the runaways almost bumped into her.

"Did you say," the old woman whispered, "that you were 'busting out'?"

Ray Joe grinned like a lynx. "The boy's idea," he said.

Jimmy reached the button for Floor One; the nurses stepped forward in unison.

"Just a minute, young man," the nurse, who had spoken to them earlier, warned.

"You see," Ray Joe said to the old woman who had now wedged herself between the nurses and the elevator, "the boy here wants to win a race, which is a lot safer than tagging bear. I want to see if I can outrun my shadow because he says it's not time for me to get tagged yet...what are you in for?"

The old woman shrugged her shoulders and leaned closer to the open elevator. In a secretive voice, she whispered: "I'm having my shadow removed—permanently!"

"Don't close that door, young man, I warn you," the nurse said.

Jimmy pressed the button and the double-doors shuddered and began to close.

"I think they're going to catch us, Granpa," he said sadly as the faces of the nurses were sealed from view.

"Our race hasn't even begun," Ray Joe retorted. From the game expression in his eyes, Jimmy took heart. But he knew what trouble waited for them on the first floor of the hospital.

"One time I heard a story about Geronimo," Ray Joe said, "he was pinned down on a mesa with cavalry all around him. And you know what he did? He sang a song to the wind. He made the wind come, and it stung the soldier's eyes, they couldn't see, and Geronimo got away."

"You know the words to his song, Granpa?"

"Press that red button, there, and I'll give it a try."

The elevator came to a throbbing halt just above the first floor.

Ray Joe began to sing:

> "The wind begins to move
> the snow starts to melt
>
> the wind on the mountains
> makes the rocks dance

the wind is coming
  a big wind
 the wind is coming
I go
  I go
In the wind
  I go."

When Ray Joe opened his eyes, they seemed to come from another place. He looked glassily around the cubicle of the elevator, his eyes resting on Jimmy.

"I don't think," he said raspily, "anyone's sung that song for better than a hundred years. . ."

Then he added, with a grin, "I know I haven't."

"What do we do now, Granpa?"

"Press any button you want, Jimmy."

Ray Joe bowed his head and folded his arms.

"I'm going to press 'B'. "

Ray Joe said nothing.

The elevator dropped swiftly, then stopped.

"Here goes," Jimmy said, pushing the Open button.

The doors yawned into a vault of darkness. For a moment Jimmy didn't know where he was. His grandfather's eyes were shut, head resting upon his chest. "We're down in the basement," Jimmy whispered, "that's where we are. . ."

Pushing the wheelchair through the aisle of cardboard boxes and packing crates, he could see a way out, a light at the end of the tunnel. The delivery door was open and pale moonlight flooded the ramp that led into the basement.

Once on that ramp, Jimmy sensed they would be safe.

"You know, Granpa, I think we just won the race."

The nurses' reception committee on the first floor of the hospital was waiting for the doors to open. When

they did, the old woman and the girl from the fourth
floor stepped out of the elevator.

"We've decided to check out of this hotel," the old
woman announced. She walked grandly up to the white
wall of nurses.

They blocked her passage, but the old woman raised
her elbows. Nimble as a dancer, she pressed on, with her
small companion in tow.

"This isn't a hotel!" the head nurse cried. "What in
blazes is going on here tonight?"

With menace in her eye, the old woman pivoted on
her heel and cocked her head at the nurse. The intent
in her eyes was like a loaded gun.

"Bye, bye, dearies."

Jimmy and Ray Joe moved rapidly down the sidewalk, out of sight of the hospital. The moon lit their way. They were making good time.

"Did I ever tell you how you got that name of yours?" Ray Joe said, yawning.

"You told me."

"That worries me."

"What does?"

"You think I could be getting . . . what's that word—senile?"

Jimmy said, "I'd like you to teach me that song sometime."

"You already know it. Come on, Jimmy, sing us home."

Jimmy sang:

> "—I go
>   I go
> in the wind
>   I go—"

The boy, the old man, and the moon rolled home, together.

Turtle
Woman

A long time ago there was a girl named Beth who lived in a country of dark woods. Beth's mother died while giving birth. Her father, a logger in that country, had been killed by a falling tree when the girl was still a child. But she had a grandmother, a solitary old Iroquois woman, who lived a life of simple seclusion by a lake in the north. After she moved in with her grandmother, all that remained of Beth's former life were a few of her father's last possessions, among them, a pair of high-laced logger's boots. These things the old lady carried up to the attic and stored with a lot of other family belongings from the past.

When Beth came to live with her grandmother, she found herself in another world. The old lady enjoyed smoking a pipe on her porch, and she was often found there, puffing contentedly, surrounded by cud-chewing goats and the neighbor's children, who liked nothing better than to ask her questions about catching woodcocks, making pets of newts, and why the maidenhair fern uncurls like a party whistle in the spring.

This new world that Beth lived in was much like a dream. Grandmother, as Beth always called her, seldom lost her temper, and she kept herself and those she cared for in a gentle world of secret thought, which, in summer, was like the spider web that pulses in the wind and, in winter, like the glaze of ice around a birch tree when the sun catches it and makes it glare.

Beth had learned from the day her father died that nothing stays. When she looked into Grandmother's eyes, she saw that one day the scrawny boys who always visited on the porch would go away and not return and the squirrels and jays they fed would come no more. She knew this as surely as she knew that Grandmother was preparing to go on the long journey her mother and father had already taken.

One morning when Grandmother seemed weaker and more distant than she had ever been before, Beth drew away from her. The time has come, she thought. But Grandmother just pulled on the ceiling ladder that led to the dusty attic. For most of that day, the old lady stayed up there stroking the soles of her dead son's logger's boots. Beth would not go up those stairs, but she heard Grandmother singing softly, and she knew this was a death song.

A day or so later, Grandmother spent several hours walking in a pine thicket near the cabin. When she returned, she told Beth, "I feel my bones are just waking up after a long sleep." Beth didn't know what to say, so she said nothing. Grandmother saw Beth draw away

and said, "Child, child. Promise me that when I'm gone, you will look for me." And her ancient eyes gazed in the direction of the pine trees.

"Where I go is a good place. Someday you will meet me there, but you must not be surprised if I do not look as I do now. For after I am gone, I will be something else, just as the winter is different from the spring. When I am gone, I would like you to bury me in that apple tree in the meadow. I planted that when I was your age and now it is the chosen place for these old bones to rest."

Beth promised that she would do this, but she drew farther and farther away until, one day, she was by herself. The days that followed were a pattern of loneliness, of learning to be alone, because Beth knew that soon it would always be that way, and she was getting ready for the day when the leaves would fall from the trees and winter would come to stay.

By the time the old woman passed away several weeks later, Beth had drawn into herself as deeply as Grandmother seemed to have come out of her own habit of solitary existence. For toward the end, the old woman sang herself to sleep at night, and in the morning Beth woke up to her sudden strange, flutelike laughter.

There wasn't a ceremony because Beth didn't know one. She carefully folded Grandmother into her most cherished blanket and carried her out to the apple tree. Then, one inch at a time, Beth hoisted her up into the first outspread branches and left her there with a poem: "Come, my friends, and dry your tears, for I will return when Christ appears."

Beth thought this little verse was something good. But she could summon no tears. There was Grandmother, asleep in the old apple tree. What difference would it make, she wondered, if Christ appeared. What could he do to bring her grandmother back to life? And even if he could, why would she wish to return? Hadn't she said she felt herself changing, turning into something?

* * * *

In the time that passed after Grandmother's death, Beth saw many things in her sleep. For a while her dreams were wild and strange. One night Grandmother came to her bedside with eyes flickering like fire coals, her face like a turtle's, eyelids droopy and full of folds. Beth saw her grandmother float about the room. The old woman's feet were webbed.

When she woke next morning, Beth got out of bed and walked barefoot to the cold island of pine at the meadow's edge. Here the woods were dense and there was little sun to light the way. She remembered the path taken by Grandmother through the pine trees. As she walked along, the briars caught on the hem of her nightdress.

A dark wandering it was, with Beth half-asleep as she wound uncertainly through the wet wood. Somewhere, the sun was up in the sky warming the day. But where she walked, the woods were dark as night with no moon. Finally she grew tired. Then she sat upon a stump and listened to the faint sobbing noise of the saw-whet owls. She felt empty inside. She had proved nothing. How far was she from the cabin? She didn't know. Nor did she know what time it was, for the pines grew so close they wove a tapestry of needles that kept out the sun.

She noticed that she could barely see herself. I am a shadow, she thought, a shadow shedding shadows in the gloom; a little girl hunting a ghost in the ghostly woods.

Then she stood up and began to walk home. That day something terrible closed between herself and the world. Something like a door that dismisses the sun as

it closes on the day. Somehow she knew there would be no more dreams.

Beth chose to live the rest of her life alone in Grandmother's cabin. Time passed slowly, as it must for all who live by themselves. Daydreaming at the window during the long winter rains, she marked those hours on earth that mattered only to her. When weather was suitable, she worked the garden, cut firewood, fed goats, repaired cedar shakes. But she lived so much by herself that after a time there was nothing she needed or wanted, she got on with her life, such as it was, and passed from girlhood to womanhood without a trace of regret. For it was all the same to her whether she was here or there, happy or sad. The boundary of her world was the ring of trees that circled the meadow.

If she tried, Beth could remember the road to town, a place to which she was completely indifferent. There were little boys she had once known who long ago had come to visit Grandmother. Though they were grown now, perhaps one or two remained who remembered her, but if they should have met, gathering wood in the forest, they would have given no sign. For Beth's eyes held the world and all things in it at one remove, and visitors to her part of the forest saw only a woman whose mysterious emptiness was nothing less than forbidding. She was one who lived apart and liked it that way.

The years fed upon the seasons. Summers flushed into autumns, winters melted into springs. Beth had

begun to get older, and in the lines of her face there was a softness that was not there before. There was a melting in her, as well as the weather, that sometimes kept her captive. Without knowing it, she slipped into that time of life when there seems to be no urgency about anything. She dreamed down the days, the seasons, until they were one to her. She was like an icicle, losing itself, one drop at a time, melting into nothing.

Nights when she slept, she did not dream. When sour wet leaves were sucked down the chimney in a sudden draft, she didn't know it. If the attic walked on itself when a strong wind came, she slept through it.

Yet there was a night, in the darkness before dawn, when a voice spoke to her. It was a voice that moved on water, a voice that came from within a cave.

"Child, have you forgotten?" the voice said.

Beth knew the voice.

"Have you gotten old?" it asked.

The voice floated on the glistening soft current of Beth's dream.

"Are you ready to meet me now?" the voice asked. Then it departed, curved in upon itself, and when Beth

woke clutching her bedclothes, she heard the rain running slantwise across the shingles.

She was sitting up in bed, staring emptily at the wall. Wasn't there something she had to do? Somewhere, in the back of her mind, waves were lapping and saying—do, do, do—like a wooden boat knocking against a dock in the wind.

She became absorbed in the rocking of the waves, rocking, rocking as she was taken back to a time in memory—to something in the attic, to a pair of old boots.

One step at a time, she climbed the ancient rungs. When her head was level with the hole in the ceiling, Beth felt something irresistible lift her into the dusty attic.

In the dim light she made out the objects of her infancy: childhood scribblings on white birchbark paper were rolled up like scrolls. There was a broken sled, a pair of sprung snowshoes. But her dead father's logging boots were gone. In their place was a pair of doeskin moccasins, which cast a cone of light into the dust and decay of the attic.

Beth reached out and touched the doeskin moccasins. They felt almost warm to the touch. Then she took them and went stiffly down the ladder. On the wide plank pine floor of the cabin, crouched in her faded nightdress, Beth put on the moccasins. They were a perfect fit—and the moment they were on her feet, she felt

young again, her blood sang with life. She closed her eyes. In her mind she saw a great bear with a fish in its paws. The fish slapped its tail, came free of the bear. Then a fishhawk fell from the sky like a dark bolt and took the fish in its talons. But, again, the fish flapped its tail and broke free, this time falling back into the stream where it was born. What this little moment of dreamtime meant, Beth did not know. But she saw the fish moving freely in the stream, safe from the two hunters of death.

"I am not going to die," she heard herself say, and then: "Oh, Grandmother. Oh, where. . .?"

The voice from the water said, "Child, do you feel your bones waking?"

"Yes," she said to herself, "Yes, I do."

Then she felt so young, so perfect in her bones, that she wanted to run across the meadow. She wanted to throw her arms to the Sun Father and shout her love. And she did—she ran out into the pine trees, smelling sweetly of sunrise, and she dreamed she was a girl again, splashing in the water of the lake, swimming like the fish she had seen behind her eyelids, swimming toward the deep dawning water of the lake.

"I'm changing," she heard herself say, but it was not her voice, it was the water's. Then she was swimming under the voice. She was riding the back of a great turtle, her fingers digging into the moss of lost summers. "Hold on, Child," the water-voice said as it took her from one dream to another into her next life.

Notes on the Stories

TURQUOISE HORSE

A true story, this happened to both my brother Sid, the illustrator of this book, and myself. We have each taught Navajo children. The issue of "sacred" versus "public domain" is often confused. Navajo stories are usually not told out of their proper season. However, I know of no other tribe as generous with their stories as the Navajo. It is my experience that The People like to share their stories, whenever appropriate, with non-Indians. Sacred stories, of which Lisa's dream may be one, are within the province of personal discretion—whether or not they may be told to an "outsider". Lisa's father's rationale is synonomous with others that I have heard; that it is the right of the individual to determine disclosure. My belief is that without sharing, we are not equal.

HAVASU SAM

The story happened in the Grand Canyon. I witnessed the leap myself. Havasu Sam is a friend I have known since the fifth grade and I credit him with helping me overcome a lifelong fear of heights. Rites of passage, in Indian and non-Indian terms, usually involve a physical act of courage. Carter Revard, an Osage poet whose work is included in the anthology *Voices of the Rainbow*, (Viking) tells a similar story in his poem called "Getting Across." A bunch of boys under a river bridge see the big garfish that lives as a two-foot black shadow in the green-brown water. When they do a "hand-over-hand" to a ledge of safety they are expressing the same pattern of transcendance as Sam and Buddy.

RUNNING GIRL

In the fall of 1988, I worked as press secretary for the Native American running team, Wings of the Southwest. The selections meet for the Cross Country National Finals in Raleigh, North Carolina, was held at Shipaulovi, Second Mesa, Hopi, Arizona. Running Girl is a real person. In Raleigh, at the Finals, I witnessed the events retold in the story, including the freak tornado. I will not forget the way the air felt the night before it struck, or the fact that Running Girl and some of her friends, unable to sleep in that warm unsavory wind, went for a late night run to work off unresolved feelings. Tribal people who have traditional beliefs are often faced with rites of passage similar to this one. The modern world imposes itself so dramatically that Indian people who have roots in the old ways, are confronted with American attitudes that are often strange, inconsistent and selfish, compared to their own lifestyle, which has, at its heart, a deep sense of communal participation in life. The tornado, for me, typified Running Girl's confrontation with white faces, white values; it rushed in, caused devastation. The race, once finished, meant little to Running Girl. The medal meant less. What was important for her was running with her friends in a national meet.

JIMMY BLUE EYES

I watched this story unfold while visiting a friend at St. Vincent's Hospital in Santa Fe. A film editor commented that the story was interesting but unrealistic because he did not believe there could be such a mixed-marriage of Pueblo-Navajo people. His comment is typical of views held by non-Indians. Jemez Pueblo has had crossovers from Navajoland since the time of the Spanish Reconquest when members of the Pueblo sought refuge from their rulers. An alliance developed that exists to this day. At a recent "Animal Dance" at Jemez, I found myself surrounded by visiting Navajos. References to hospital body removal may be found in Clyde Kluckhohn and Dorothy Leighton's classic work, *The Navajo*, Doubleday Anchor. References to Navajo death and burial rites may also be found in Tony Hillerman's excellent *The Ghostway*. People have asked whether Navajos today fear ghosts and if hospitals still assume the task of "body-removal" for families not wishing to have contact with the dead. Jimmy Blue Eyes is based on a particular family rather than a general one. The family is divided because the Navajo side, the matriarchal or ruling part, is old fashioned. The ghost fear does exist on the reservation today, but perhaps not to the degree that it once did.

TURTLE WOMAN

A less mystical version of Grandmother was my great aunt. Staying with with her one summer, my brother and I, paddling a canoe in the swamp, came across the Old Man of the Lake, a giant snapping turtle, who, according to local legend, took the dying to their final resting place.

There was, around 1920, a real girl who resembled Beth. My mother found her grave in a grove of pines near the lake in western Massachusetts. On the faded and worn stone there was a poem, the one that Beth recites after she enshrines Grandmother in the apple tree.

In the early 1960's I met a man who lived on the same lake who remembered, as a very young boy, finding a grove of pines near the edge of the swamp. In one of the trees, he discovered a skeleton, half-grown into the trunks of pine. He called it an "Indian burial," but whether it was or not, didn't interest me as much as the fact that the swamp, which had always haunted us as children, was full of dark and fabulous lore. That others had encountered it, as well as our family, was strangely reassuring.

Turtle Woman is a mystical story of life after death, based on Native American legends about the return to the world of the spirit. Beth tries to find Grandmother after she is gone, but she is too much a part of the world to find that place where the spirits dwell. I actually believe there are geographical planes where the two worlds meet in a kind of harmonium. The lake in the pines, the one where we grew up, might be one of those.

A book that deals with the return to a mystical place of origin is *When the Legends Die* (Bantam) by Hal Borland. The author, whom I met some years before his death, told me that his boyhood memories took him back to the forest where Thomas Black Bull, the Ute protagonist of the novel, meets the giant bear who was his childhood friend. When my great aunt died, close to the place where I first encountered the Old Man of the Lake, she said: "We are part Indian, and you are welcome to it." I didn't fully understand what she meant until I read *When the Legends Die*, the story of an Indian who lives in two worlds.

It is always a wonder to me, that there are tribal people who can and do adhere to the old, good ways and yet live in this puzzling time of shifting values.

The Publisher

Mariposa Printing & Publishing was established in 1980. Our goal is to provide quality-crafted, limited edition publications in various literary fields.

Your comments and suggestions are appreciated. Contact Joe Mowrey, owner-production manager, Mariposa Printing & Publishing, 922 Baca Street, Santa Fe, New Mexico, (505) 988-5582.

The Author

Gerald Hausman is a teacher, editor and writer who lives outside Santa Fe, New Mexico. He spends part of each year storytelling and presenting workshops throughout the United States.

The Illustrator

Sid Hausman has lived in New Mexico for 25 years. A graduate of Highlands University, he is part of an era in which the school produced many of the renowned artists in Santa Fe today. He is known for his work in leather and jewelry, as well as music and illustration. For the past 10 years, Sid has been a resident artist with the New Mexico Arts Division, teaching songwriting at Navajo and pueblo schools including Zuni, Jemez, and Santo Domingo. In his songwriting workshops, he will often have the kids illustrate their visual interpretations of the songs.

Sid Hausman's earlier broadsides and illustrations have been published by the Gilgia Press, Lawrence Hill and Co., Bear and Co., and Sunstone Press. He currently resides with his wife Cappie, in Tesuque, New Mexico.